FEARLESS FITZROY

Kathy Henderson has written and illustrated many children's books. Her picture books include *The Storm*, which was shortlisted for the Kate Greenaway Medal; *And the Good Brown Earth*; *The Little Boat*, illustrated by Patrick Benson, which won the Kurt Maschler Award and was shortlisted for the Smarties Book Prize; and *The Year in the City*, illustrated by Paul Howard. She has also written a number of fiction titles for older children. Kathy has three children and lives in London.

KATHY HENDERSON

Fearless Fitzroy

Illustrations by Alex Merry

WALKER BOOKS
AND SUBSIDIARIES
LONDON · BOSTON · SYDNEY · AUCKLAND

*For Megan, Alice and Piccolini
and, of course, for Silver*

First published 2005 by Walker Books Ltd
87 Vauxhall Walk, London SE11 5HJ

2 4 6 8 10 9 7 5 3 1

Text © 2005 Kathy Henderson
Illustrations © 2005 Alex Merry

The right of Kathy Henderson and Alex Merry to be identified
as author and illustrator respectively of this work has been asserted
by them in accordance with the Copyright, Designs and Patents Act 1988

This book has been typeset in Garamond

Printed in Great Britain by J.H. Haynes & Co. Ltd

British Library Cataloguing in Publication Data:
a catalogue record for this book
is available from the British Library

ISBN 1-84428-633-9

www.walkerbooks.co.uk

Contents

Chapter One

Fearless Fitzroy Mouser was a laid-back cat.

He slept. He dozed. He stretched. He snoozed.

He lazed. He purred. He barely stirred.

He yawned and sighed, sometimes opened one eye, but only got up to eat his food.

The rest of the time he lazed and dozed while the dust piled up on the end of his nose.

Nothing disturbed Fitzroy: not noise, not rats, not shocks, or shadows. Fitzroy was fearless. Well, almost.

But there was just one nightmare, the nightmare every cat grows up to dread, which could make him sweat and shake with terror. It was the nightmare of the …

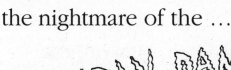

"NO NO NO NO NO!" Fitzroy would whimper as the terrible dangling creature with its pointy nose, its eyes on stalks and its huge, sharp, biting teeth made him shudder and twitch. "It's only a dream." And he'd roll over and try to go on sleeping.

Now Fitzroy lived and worked
(if you can call it work) in a big
dry warehouse full of **Famous
Chocolate Biscuits**. His job
was to keep out birds and rats,
insects and bats, but most of all
mice – mice, mice, mice – especially
the chocolate-biscuit-eating kind.

For this he got two good meals
a day, regular as clockwork.
In return, did Fitzroy hunt and
pounce and guard the stores?

Absolutely not!
Fitzroy snoozed.

Mouse parents for miles around thought Fitzroy was just perfect for cat practice.

They brought their children along in rows to teach them what every young mouse needs to know about cats. (And to feast on chocolate biscuits.)

And mouse children for miles around longed to be big enough to see Fearless Fitzroy for themselves. But big enough they had to be. "When your ears touch the top of the mousehole and your paws reach from side to side, *then* you can go, but not before." That was the rule.

Chapter Two

Among the many mouse parents living near the **Famous Chocolate Biscuits** warehouse were two sisters: Meza and Milla Mouse. They lived in neighbouring nests and between them they had so many children, they could scarcely keep track.

Meza had eleven mouselets and
Milla had twelve – well, that's what
she always said – but *in fact* Milla
had thirteen. It was just
that the smallest of the
litter, Piccolini by
name, was so skinny
and small that she
didn't really count.

Piccolini was tiny. She had small bright eyes, a very small nose and an even smaller squeak. She  had puny little legs, a thread of a tail and grey fur so pale she was almost invisible. And as she tripped over her big baby feet in the rumpus of all her brothers and sisters and cousins, nobody even noticed she was there.

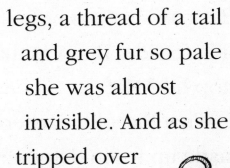

19

How Piccolini longed to be big! She did everything she could to catch up with her brothers and sisters and cousins, but it was no good. Her ears were never going to touch the top of the mousehole. Her paws would never reach from side to side. But was that going to stop her? No!

What Piccolini lacked in size, she made up for in determination. So  when at last the day came when all the other mouselets were big enough to go and see Fearless Fitzroy, Piccolini was ready.

As they all lined up to do the mousehole test, she jumped up under the belly of her biggest, sturdiest brother and hid away in his thick, soft fur until they were safely through. And did anybody notice? Of course not.

Chapter Three

That morning at the biscuit
warehouse seemed much the same
as any other. When Fitzroy opened
one lazy eye there was nothing to
keep him awake. And as Meza, Milla
and the mouse children set out along
the runs and tunnels towards him,
nothing looked unusual.

But this was a day with a difference because, without any warning, the owner of the warehouse, the King of the Chocolate Biscuits, the Provider of the Cat Food, the Boss Fitzroy had never met, MR FAME himself, paid an unexpected visit!

Mr Fame was a very busy man. He had five motor cars, four offices, three houses, two yachts, one private plane and, oh yes, the **Famous Chocolate Biscuits** empire to run.

As long as everything ran smoothly he didn't bother himself with what went on in his warehouse. In fact, it wasn't clear that he'd ever *been* to his warehouse before. But recently complaints had started to reach him from smart shops around the world. They complained about biscuits with holes in the middle and nibbles round the edges, about biscuits with paw prints in the chocolate and tooth marks on the wrappers. And Mr Fame decided it was time to act.

So on this very morning, as Meza and Milla and all the little mouse children were setting out, he swept down to Fitzroy's home in his chauffeur-driven limousine to take a look for himself.

Mr Fame looked hard. He noticed the mess. He noticed the mouse droppings. He noticed the open crates and the leaky packets and the trail of biscuit crumbs and chocolate chips all over the floor.

And then he noticed Fitzroy, who, of course, didn't notice anything at all, because he was fast asleep and snoring as usual.

"I might have guessed!" he thundered. "Sloppy staff! Bad management! THAT CAT WILL HAVE TO GO!" And punching the number of **CAT KILLERS INCORPORATED** angrily into his mobile phone he stormed out.

Chapter Four

The dust had barely settled behind
Mr Fame's car when Meza and
Milla counted their mouselets into
the warehouse through a hole in
the floor. "One, two, three …
eleven … fifteen … twenty-two,
twenty-three. Good."

"And me!" squeaked
Piccolini, jumping up
and down – but
nobody noticed.

There in front of them lay the
mighty Fitzroy, huge and snoring.

"Oh wow!" breathed the
mouselets. "OH WOW!"

"Right," said Milla, arranging them in rows. "Now, pay attention, because this is possibly the *most important* lesson of your *whole lives…*"

And as Meza took up position by Fitzroy's side, Milla climbed up on a packet of **Famous Chocolate Biscuits** and began.

"ITEM ONE," she squeaked as Meza rolled one of Fitzroy's big paws over. "Inside these soft paws there are claws sharp as knives. If you give them a chance they will cut off your lives!

"ITEM TWO: mouth and jaws. Very big teeth in there. They'll crunch you up, so mice BEWARE!

31

"ITEM THREE," said Milla as Meza lifted one of Fitzroy's eyelids. "These are eyes, cat-size spies that can see in the dark. Little mice, if you're wise: hide! Don't get spied.

"ITEM FOUR," as Meza wrapped Fitzroy's tail around her neck like a fake fur collar. "A tail tells you a lot. If you once see it flick, you know a cat's angry – so mice get out quick!"

On went the lesson. The little mice listened, eyes wide, deeply impressed to find themselves so close to such a huge and dangerous creature.

Most of them listened, anyway. But Piccolini was dozing off. All that running had tired her out, even though she'd hitched a ride on one of her big sisters' tails for the last part of the journey. Now she found it hard to concentrate. She found it hard to stay awake. The lesson droned on and on and...

"What is the single most
important thing to remember about
cats?" asked Milla at last.

The little mice waved their tails
in the air.

"WHISKERS!" they squeaked. All
except Piccolini,
who was fast
asleep.

"That's right! Well done! And what's the one rule you must NEVER forget?"

"Don't touch. Stay clear. And *NEVER EVER PULL* A CAT'S WHISKERS!"

This time they yelled so loudly that Piccolini was jolted wide awake.

"What? What!" she squeaked. But nobody noticed.

Chapter Five

At last the lesson was over. Milla jumped down from the biscuit packet she'd been standing on and helped Meza to tip it over onto its side. With a zip of their razor mice teeth they had the shiny wrapper off and the **Famous** scrunchy, crunchy, sticky, licky **Chocolate Biscuits** slid out onto the floor.

This was the bit all the little mice had been been waiting for. What a feast!

What crumbs and deliciousness! Their little tails wiggled in delight as they munched and they gnawed and they gobbled until every last biscuit had gone. And all this barely three tail lengths from Fearless Fitzroy Mouser's sleeping nose!

Meza and Milla were now very full and rather sleepy themselves. Not so the little mice. They were bursting with chocolate energy.

"Mmmmm," said Meza as she cleaned her whiskers. "Now run along and play." And she settled down for a lazy chat with her sister.

The mouse children set off to
explore the biggest, best and furriest
adventure playground ever – FITZROY!

They swarmed up his sleeping
back. They tobogganed down his
sleeping sides. They swung from his
sleeping ears. They used his
tail as a skipping rope
and played hide-and-
seek under his
sleeping
paws.

They were just dancing the conga
in a great long line up his back and
over his head, each little mouse
holding the tail of the one in front
and kicking out their little legs in a
stomping rhythm, when …

… the door of the warehouse flew
open with a **CLANG!** and there
stood the boss, Mr Fame himself!

This time he had someone with
him …

… a heavy man in big gloves wearing baggy overalls with the words **CAT KILLERS INCORPORATED** printed on the back. In one hand he had a big stick and in the other a large black sack.

"JUST GET RID OF HIM!" Mr Fame was bellowing. "I don't care how. It's time for mousetraps."

Chapter Six

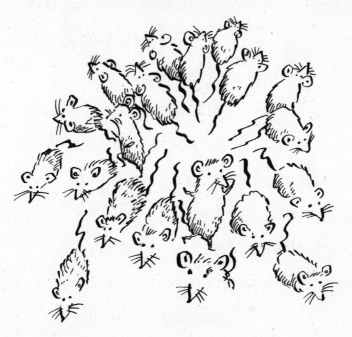

For a split second everyone froze.
Oh no! Not Fitzroy! Not mousetraps!
Not that! Then, in the blink of an
eye, the twitch of a tail, both mother
mice and all twenty-three mouselets
simply vanished.

Only tiny Piccolini
was left, frozen to
the spot on top of
Fearless Fitzroy's
snoozing head with
a look of
horror on her face.
Suddenly she lost
her balance. She
teetered, she tottered

and, with
a piercing
shriek right into
Fitzroy's ear, she
toppled straight over
his eye and fell into
space, paws flailing.

And then she did something terrible, something every mouse knows you should never do (but then she'd missed that bit of the lesson). She broke the one rule of cat safety no mouse must ever forget!

SHE GRABBED HOLD OF A WHISKER

… and hung there, suspended in mid-air, eyes on stalks, mouth wide open.

Piccolini's shriek tore into
Fitzroy's dream with deafening
force. An instant later a terrible stab
of pain from the tip of his nose to
the end of his tail hurtled him
awake. His head swung back,
his eyes snapped open and –
Oh no! Oh YES! – Fearless Fitzroy
found himself face to face with his
very worst nightmare,
every cat's
greatest fear,

the DEADLY
DANGLING
MOUSE
MONSTER
itself!

It was big, it was ugly, it had eyes
on stalks and huge, sharp, biting teeth
and … OH! OH! OH! HOW IT HURT!

49

Fitzroy leapt into the air. He
roared and he clawed. He snarled
and he howled. He lashed and he
smashed and he spun and he ran.

50

Like the greatest mouse-mangling hunter in the world, oh, how he fought, until little Piccolini (who was so small nobody really noticed her) lost her grip on the whisker she was clinging to as she dangled right there **WHAM!** in front of Fitzroy's eyes and was hurled across the warehouse like a piece of thistledown.

Frantic Fitzroy
was so busy
springing up in
the air and
landing **BANG!**
on all four feet,
snarling and
scratching and fighting, that for a
split second he didn't realize what
had happened. Then it dawned on
him. It was over! The DEADLY
DANGLING MOUSE MONSTER
had gone! He had shaken it off!
He had won!

Chapter Seven

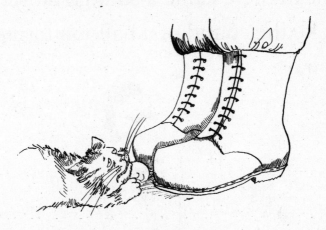

With a howl of relief Fitzroy came to a stop, chest heaving, in front of a pair of heavy studded boots, an evil-smelling sack and a bloodstained club.

"You sure you want to get rid of him, boss?" said a voice. "He looks like a champion mouser to me. Still, if you say so…" And the heavy club swung slowly up into the air.

From somewhere above Fitzroy's head there came a strange noise, like the sound of a balloon losing air.

It was Mr Fame.

He didn't like being made to look silly, certainly not by a cat, even less by a cat disposal man. He gawped like a goldfish, puffed like a kettle.

"STOP!" he exploded at last.
"Get rid of him? Of course not!
What ever gave you that idea?
Mousetraps? Ridiculous! You must
be a fool! As for parting with this
fine beast" – waving at Fitzroy –
"I wouldn't dream of it! Essential!
Senior management!" And on and
on he went, getting more and more
indignant.

At this point Fitzroy lost interest. Out of the corner of his eye he could see something moving, something very small.

Fitzroy stared. There, dancing along the skirting board, tripping over her big baby feet and grinning at him, was the tiniest mouse he'd ever seen … a mouse who looked strangely familiar … like a miniature version of… Surely not!!! Oh yes! The DEADLY DANGLING MOUSE MONSTER!

Slowly Fitzroy
began to blush.
From the tip of
his tail to the top
of his nose he
blushed, not that
anyone could tell
with all that fur, except

possibly Piccolini. But
she was looking
straight at him
with one paw to
her lips and the
other pointing up
over his head to
where Mr Fame was
dancing with rage.

And as Mr Fame, still shouting, pushed the cat disposal man out of the warehouse and slammed the door, Fitzroy sank to the ground with a sigh of relief. If you'd been listening carefully you would have heard an answering whispery sigh of relief echo all round the warehouse and out of every mousehole.

But the only mouse you'd have noticed would have been Piccolini as she blew Fitzroy a kiss and winked.

As for Mr Fame, he never set foot
in the warehouse again, although
he sent parcels of pilchards and
salmon to Fitzroy addressed to
The Senior Mouse Manager. Soon
afterwards **Famous Chocolate
Biscuits** introduced a new
trademark. It was the print of
a mouse's foot in chocolate. **Want
the best? Look for the paw print!**
said the label.

Fearless Fitzroy,
who was now
not afraid of
anything at all,
slept better than
ever before.

And Piccolini? Well, she never grew very big, but overnight she became, without a doubt, the most famous mouse for miles around.

From that time on she spent her days in the biscuit warehouse watching over her big friend as he snoozed. And she made very sure that all the little mice who came to do their cat practice never ruffled a single whisker.

other **sprinters** for you to enjoy!

Taking the Cat's Way Home
Jan Mark • Paul Howard

New boy William seems to have it in for Jane, and the only way she can escape him after school is to follow her cat along the wall, into the unknown…

Care of Henry
Anne Fine • Paul Howard

When Hugo's mum goes into hospital, he must decide who he wants to stay with. The key to it all is Henry, his dog.

The Finger-Eater
Dick King-Smith • Arthur Robins

Long ago, in the cold lands of the North, there lived a troll named Ulf, who had a very bad habit – he liked to eat fingers!

Cool as a Cucumber
Michael Morpurgo • Tor Freeman

Peter gets more than he bargained for when he starts digging the school's Jubilee vegetable garden!

Star Striker Titch
Martin Waddell • Russell Ayto

Little Titch wants to play a big part in the school World Cup – if only he could get on the pitch!